1 Lee Road City Farm

"I've only met a hen once. It bit the top off my finger," said Kate.

"Of course it didn't," said her mother. "It gave you a little peck, that's all."

"There was blood," said Kate.

"Not much," said her mother, folding back the page of the local newspaper so that the article about the City Farm was at the top.

"There shouldn't have been any," said Kate. "You're not supposed to see your own blood."

"It didn't mean any harm," said her mother, who thought life went along better if you believed the best of everyone. "You frightened it."

"I don't see how I could have," said Kate. "It was

bigger than me."

"Are you sure it was a hen?" said her father, looking faintly alarmed.

"She was only two," said her mother. "You know what she was like at that age. She tried to put her finger in its nostril."

"Why don't I remember this killer-hen?" said her father. He had three hobbies – growing plants from pips, swimming and worrying that Kate might get into some sort of danger. Normally, she wouldn't have told him the hen story.

"You were off on one of your courses and we were staying with Grandma," said her mother, who also had three hobbies – taking photographs, swimming and trying to stop everybody worrying about anything. "You'll find hens look quite small now, Kate."

Kate's father sold computer systems to large firms, and the courses he went on were either about new kinds of computers, new ways of persuading people to buy computers or both at once. It was because of the computer systems that Kate's mother was trying to get her interested in Lee Road City Farm. Her father had, quite unexpectedly, been given a new area to sell the systems in. At the same time he had been told that the family would have to pack up and move to this new area.

They didn't particularly want to live somewhere different, but none of them could think of a good enough reason not to, so they did. The different house was all right, and had a suitable windowsill for the pip plants. The different hospital had a job for Kate's mother, teaching people who'd broken bits of themselves how to move around again. The different school was fine. But now, for some reason, Kate's mother had decided that Kate needed more friends than she would meet at school, and that Lee Road Farm was the place to find them.

"I don't want to be sent to work on a farm," said Kate, in the most pathetic voice she could manage. "I'm too young."

"I hope you don't say things like that to other people," said her mother, rustling the paper. "I'm not 'sending you to work' anywhere. I think it would be fun for you to join the Junior Farmers' Club, that's all. I doubt if Junior Farmers work at all, I should think they just play with the animals."

Her father was sitting across the room with a map of the area and a pen, marking the places he had to visit next day. He drew a neat circle near the top and said, "I don't see how city people can run a farm." He came from a small town, where Grandma still lived, and he liked to think he was a bit of a

countryman. He knew significant things about herbs, and when he had a headache he made himself a drink of boiling water and dried daisies which he said was better than aspirin. Though sometimes he took an aspirin at the same time, just to be on the safe side.

"Well, let's go and have a look," said Kate's mother. "See if we think they're doing it right."

"It's Sunday," said Kate, who was leaning on the back of the sofa and reading the article over her mother's shoulder. "You can only be a Junior Farmer on a Saturday. It says."

"It also says visitors are welcome to look round any day," said her mother. "Except Mondays when it's shut."

"How on earth can you shut a farm?" said her father. "Where's the stock supposed to go on Mondays?"

"Shut to visitors, I mean," said her mother. "Not to the people who feed the animals. Why do you both have to be so negative? Come on, it's only about three roads away."

"I don't see how it can be," said her father, frowning at his map. "It must be on the outskirts somewhere. There's nothing but streets and buildings around here, except where the railway line cuts through. The only large-ish open space is on the industrial estate, and that's a car park."

"There's a funny little diagram at the end of this article," said her mother, "which shows the farm between us and the railway viaduct."

"Someone's made a mistake," said her father. "There can't be fields down there. No room."

Kate's mother jumped up, flung the newspaper down on the sofa, and said, "Oh, for goodness' sake, get yourselves together you two, and let's go out and see. It'll take us about four and a quarter minutes to walk to where it's supposed to be. That's not a very big hole in either of your lives, is it?"

"I'll come and look once," said Kate guardedly. "But if anything bites me, I'm not going again."

2 Cleopatra the Beautiful

It was quite true there were no fields.

Following the diagram in the paper, they walked down a road with derelict buildings on one side and a long block of flats with small shops underneath them on the other. Ahead they saw a high wire mesh fence, curved inwards at the top in true maximum-security style. Towards the right-hand end of this fence was a padlocked wire gate with a sign hanging on it which read 'LEE ROAD FARM'. Some way beyond the fence stood the dirty brick railway viaduct, and even as they looked a goods train clattered slowly and noisily across the top of it. Their view of whatever lay between the fence and the viaduct was blocked by a couple of shed-like buildings to the left of the gate. To the right was a patch of shorn grass and an old abandoned rug piled up against the mesh.

Even Kate's mother slowed down a bit.

"Whatever used to be there, it's locked up and forgotten now," said her father.

"It's supposed to be very new," said her mother. "According to the article."

Kate, who was walking a bit ahead of them, could see further. "The padlock isn't shut," she said. "It's just hanging there."

Her parents followed her across the road to the fence, and then two things happened at the same time. One was that the noise of the train died away and they all heard, quite clearly, the sound of hens.

The other was that the abandoned rug turned its head to look at them, and then bleated in a not-unfriendly way. The sheep was lying with her back jammed comfortably against the fence, but when Kate tried to stroke the bits of creamy wool that bulged through the squares, she turned her head away, bored.

"She probably can't feel a thing," said her father, "through all that wool. I'm surprised they haven't shorn her yet. And where on earth is she supposed to graze?"

Kate, who couldn't work out where the hens were, slid the bolt back without quite meaning to, pushed the gate open and walked in. Her parents followed, her father clanking the bolt loudly behind them and muttering about the importance of shutting farm gates properly.

The sheep watched them without further comment.

Once past the two shed-like buildings they were in an unexpectedly large space, though still small by the standards of a country farm. After the huge outer fence, it was a surprise to see that there were hardly any inner ones.

Facing them at the far side of the farmyard was a line of low buildings, most of them wooden but one made of brick, with a proper door and windows and a brick outhouse at the side. Next to that there were two small stables, both with the doors open.

Off by themselves, to the right of these, were two more wooden enclosures, one of which seemed to contain a lot of banging and shrill, excited cries.

Way over to the left, away from the buildings, there was a low, makeshift fence around a scrubby weedy area with a bucket in it. Beside the bucket stood three geese, with long indignant necks, watching.

Right in the middle, and entirely by itself, was a single, impressive wooden fence with a gate in it. This gate was latched, which seemed rather unnecessary since the other three sides of fence were missing.

Apart from the bit of grass they'd seen from the gate, most of the ground was stony earth. What they could see of it. A man with a bucket had just strewn a brightly coloured mixture far and wide − red carrot stubs, green cabbage stalks, bits of yellow turnip, scatterings of corn, and some dry-looking brownish things which couldn't have been pebbles or the sheep wouldn't have been eating them.

As well as the sheep dozing by the gate, there were four more like her, two of them a bit smaller and with shorter coats which Kate decided must be oldish lambs. Easy to see where the hens were now. Two of them were perched on the back of one of the sheep, who didn't seem to mind. Two were on the fence, looking self-satisfied. The rest were busy scuffing and beaking at the ground, among the feet of the pebble-eating sheep, and of the goats who were chewing at everything else.

There were three nanny goats, each tethered to a

stake in the ground, two of them with blotchy brown-and-white coats, and a shaggy blonde one. And there were three goat kids, one to match each nanny. The kids, who were not tied up, were playing tug-of-war with cabbage stalks, their thin little legs braced.

As Kate looked, one of the blotchy goat kids separated itself from the rest. It bounced over to her on tiny hard hooves, as though it was wearing miniature high-heeled shoes, gave her a look of overwhelming affection out of its strange eyes, planted its front feet on her stomach and began to eat her belt.

"Just shove her off, don't be nervous," called the man with the bucket. To her surprise, Kate realised she wasn't nervous. She pulled her belt-end out of the busily nibbling mouth, elbowed the kid aside, and bent down to pick up a cabbage stalk. "Try this," she said. "Better for you." The kid accepted it without complaining.

The man with the bucket came over. "Nice to see you," he said to all three of them in general. "We don't get many visitors yet. We've not been open very long."

He had thick hair and a thick beard but no moustache, so that his face seemed to have a curly brown frame around it. It made him look very much like a monkey glove-puppet Kate had been extremely fond of when she was younger. She started to tell him so, then decided that he might not wish to know. So she changed it to, "I like your beard."

"Kate!" said her mother. "Don't make personal remarks."

But the man said, "Oh thank you. I think the animals do, too. I feel we look more normal to them if we're as hairy as possible."

Kate's father raised his eyes to the sky, but didn't speak. The goat kid bobbed away to inspect a carrot. A tall boy of about fifteen appeared from behind the small stables and called, "Mike, shall I let the geese out?"

At the same time, Kate's mother said, "We've come to enquire about the Junior Farmers' Club."

"Oh, right," said Mike, dumping the bucket. "Come in to the office." Then, more loudly, "Yes, thanks Dan."

Kate's parents followed Mike across the big yard into the main building. Kate stayed outside and watched the kids, who were wagging their tiny tails like dogs and playing like puppies; two blotchy flop-eared ones and a shaggy blonde. Then one of the blotchy flop-eared nanny goats raised her head, still chewing, and looked straight at Kate. Kate decided she was the mother of the kid who had tried to eat her belt.

"Hallo," said Kate.

The goat gazed at her and took a few steps nearer, then stopped because her rope wouldn't stretch any further. Her long ears, drooping down each side of her long brown and white face, gave her a calm, relaxed look. Also, she seemed to be smiling.

"You're beautiful," said Kate, and she took a few steps forward, too, so that they met.

The goat lowered her head and pushed the top of it firmly against Kate's chest. It wasn't like being

butted, or shoved; it felt friendly. Kate stroked the coarse head hair and then pulled very gently on the flop-ears. The goat looked into her face. It didn't seem much shorter than she was.

"Goats are supposed to be white, and they have horns and little beards," said Kate. "Why aren't you white?"

"Because she's an Anglo-Nubian," said Mike, unexpectedly, at her side. "That's Cleopatra. The other Anglo-Nubian is her niece, Charmian. And Blondie, over there, is a Golden Guernsey."

"I like Cleopatra," said Kate.

"She likes you," said Mike. "When you join us you can learn to milk her."

Kate thought about that and decided it was a nice idea.

"She can't join us," said Dan. He'd opened the goose-gate and walked up to join them. "There's a bottom age-limit for the Club, don't forget. You can see she's too young."

That was what Kate had said herself, but it didn't sound so good coming from someone else. "Doesn't anyone as young as me come?" she asked Dan.

"Only in supervised groups or with their parents," said Dan dismissively.

Before Kate could think of anything to say, a girl of about Dan's age appeared from nowhere, dragging a garden rake behind her. "I've prepared the bed," she said to Mike, whatever that meant. Then, to Dan, "Don't be so mean. We need all the help we can get. Why shouldn't she come along?"

"She's too young," Dan said again, with a shrug.

"Well, she'll grow out of that, won't she," said the girl. "I bet Jenny would let her join."

"I did promise she could milk Cleopatra," said Mike, looking fussed.

Kate said nothing because at that moment she saw a movement out of the corner of her eye and heard her father shout her name from the office in a higher-pitched voice than usual. She turned quickly

and saw a goose, its neck stretched out as long as it would go, running straight for her, at considerable speed. There was no smile on its beak, no kind look in its angry little eye. Kate ran.

She didn't stop until she got to the mesh gate. Then, just before opening it, she looked behind her. There was no sign of the goose, but a certain amount of scuffling and shouting was going on behind the barrier of sheds.

With extreme caution, Kate let go of the gate-bolt, sidled slowly back into the farmyard and peered round the outside wall of the nearest shed. The girl was shutting the geese back in their pen, Mike was walking away from the goose-pen towards the office, Dan was laughing, her mother was looking startled, her father was looking stern.

"NOW do you believe she's too young?" said Dan. "It's useless running away from him, it only encourages him."

"She did the right thing," said Mike firmly. "He's in a mean mood today, which isn't very surprising because he's in a mean mood most days." He patted Kate on the shoulder. "It's nice to meet a new neighbour," he said. "You're welcome to join us."

"Only if she wants to," said her mother quickly.

"She doesn't want to," said her father, just as quickly.

"Course she wants to," said the girl.

Dan just snorted.

Kate, who was still a little out of breath, gathered together all the dignity she could find. "I'll come next Saturday," she said, "and milk Cleopatra. After that, I probably shan't bother any more."

3 Do People Milk Sheep?

Kate's father insisted on walking with her to the farm on Saturday afternoon. If someone already thinks you're too young for something, it isn't helpful to turn up with one of your parents, and Kate tried hard to shake him off at the gate. He walked right on in, though, and was impressed to see that the pen in the centre had already been finished off, with stout fencing on its remaining three sides. The goat kids were in there, and someone had made a complicated structure out of three packing cases, two planks and a broken chair for them to climb and slide on. The adult goats were penned into their little stables beside the office, looking out over their half-doors. Cleopatra seemed to wink at Kate, but that might have been her imagination.

The girl who had taken Kate's side on the first day, and who turned out to be called Alison, was with Mike near the goose-pen when Kate and her father arrived. She came straight up to them and led Kate away, leaving her father to talk knowledgeably to Mike about the price of sheep-feed and the importance of Council Grants. "You didn't see round properly last time," she said, "what with your parents and Gander."

"A gander," said Kate apologetically. "I thought it was a goose."

"He IS a gander," said Alison, "but he's also called Gander. It just seemed the right name for him. Would you like to see the pigs?"

"I didn't know there were pigs," said Kate, and then remembered something. "Was that what all the banging and squealing was?"

"I should think so," said Alison, leading the way to the two wooden enclosures at the far right end. "They're quiet now, they've just been fed."

"Phooo!" said Kate, as they reached the first enclosure.

"And they're just about to be cleaned out," said

Alison, as Dan and another boy appeared from behind the sties, wearing gumboots and carrying buckets and brooms. Kate wasn't sure if she was entirely pleased to see Dan, so she hung over the gate of the sty and gazed down at the sow who was sleeping breathily, her bristly sides rising and falling, her ears curved down over her eyes as if to keep out the light.

"And here's her litter," said Alison, guiding her to the next sty.

"Aaaaaaah!" said Kate, and then wished she hadn't because Dan immediately imitated her.

The piglets were all at the front of their sty, lying together in a mixed-up heap. As she watched, one got up, reversed away from the rest, and then

wriggled into the group again, first shoving its snout into a tiny gap between two of the others, and then pushing in as much of the rest of its body as it could.

Just as Kate had always known that goats were white until she met Cleopatra, so she had always known that pigs were pink until she stared down at these, which were whitish with a few blackish splotches.

"They're Gloucester Old Spots," said Alison. "See the markings? Makes them easier to tell apart."

"I'll give you their names," said Dan, beside her. "The sow is Abigail, and these" – he pointed at different bits of the sleeping heap in turn – "are Abel, Amelia, Arnold, Amy, Alban, Aylmer, Ada and Adeline. We wanted to call one Alison, but she wouldn't let us."

"They're our first litter," said Alison, ignoring him, "so we've given them all A names. The next lot'll be Bs."

"I'll be testing you on the names later," said Dan to Kate. "I hope you were paying attention."

Kate stared anxiously at the litter. No chance, she thought. If I can't even see how many there are, I'm not likely to be able to tell them apart.

"No point you two getting stuck into the mucking out yet," said Alison, reaching down to scratch Abigail's ear. The sow smiled in her sleep and made a grumbling noise of pleasure. "Jenny's holding a meeting as soon as everyone's here. We may as well get that out of the way first. Seth, do you want to round up people from the allotment?"

The other boy went off behind the sties and Alison followed him as far as the corner. "Here," she said to Kate, "here's the rest of it – so far."

From the back of the buildings it was possible to see as far as the viaduct, whose great arch gaped darkly at them. This bit of stony earth was bigger than the farmyard. Round the edges there were shrubby bushes and some tall straggly plants that were very likely weeds. Roughly in the middle, a small patch had been dug out and planted in neat rows. Beside it stood a curved plastic tent which Alison said was a makeshift greenhouse. Two girls and a boy, all a bit older than Kate, were collecting stones from the earth near the beds and putting them in piles. Seth had already reached them and was pointing back towards the main building.

"There's a lot to do," said Alison. "We hardly grow anything yet. Just some salad stuff. But we have big plans. Vegetables, soft fruit, a proper herb garden."

"Mum thinks Junior Farmers just play with the animals," said Kate.

"Oh no! We work," said Alison. "Come on, after the meeting someone will find you a job."

"You'd better not let her collect the eggs," said Seth, catching up with them. "She'll probably try to put them back in the hens."

Oh, thought Kate, Dan's not my only enemy, and she looked warily at the group of stone-gatherers as they all went in to the office.

The one they called Jenny was already inside. It turned out later that she was married to Mike, and she obviously shared his opinion about hair. Hers,

which was dark, reached down to her waist, though
it was pulled back into a rubber band with a gold
button on it. She sat on the edge of the big table and
smiled. Mike, Alison, Dan and a man they called
George stood around leaning on things. Seth, the
three stone-gatherers and Kate sat on the floor.
Kate's father, she was glad to notice, was not there
any more, although she thought she wouldn't mind
too much if he turned up at the end, in case she
couldn't remember the way home.

"Right," said Jenny. "We've got some exciting
news."

Everyone made polite enthusiastic noises.

"But it's going to mean a lot of hard work."

Everyone moaned and sighed and flopped about,
but none of them looked as though they seriously
minded.

"And I'm telling the groups of volunteers this week because we're going to need all the help we can get. First of all" – Jenny paused for maximum effect – "we've been offered a pony."

There was a cheer that was real, rather than polite, from everyone but Kate, who felt a bit out of her depth. The goats seemed friendly, the pigs were often asleep, the hens were small enough, the sheep kept themselves to themselves, and the geese and Gander were behind a fence – but a pony. She wasn't sure what problems that might bring her.

"The pony – Polka – needs a new home," Jenny went on, "because her young owner has outgrown her and will be going on to something a bit bigger. The reason she's on offer to us is because her owner's grandfather, Mr Sedgwick, used to live here. I mean exactly here," and she pointed at the floor of the office. "He lived in a house on this site until he was bombed out during the Second World War. The back wall of this office and of the dairy were part of his house. They were still standing, so we built on to them."

Everyone looked respectfully at the back wall of the office, which was unpainted brickwork with two windows and a row of cupboards standing against it.

"The bombers were aiming for the railway line," said Jenny, "but they got the houses as well. This land remained pretty much derelict for all those years until we took it over − unless you count the time it was a used car lot. Mr Sedgwick was so pleased to hear about us that as soon as he knew the pony had to go, he wrote to say he wanted us to have her. And that's not all . . ." She paused and smiled around at them. "Polka comes as part of a package with an inseparable friend of hers, a donkey called Dot."

There were more cheers, though Dan sighed noisily.

"Yes, Dan," said Jenny, "names are always a bit of a trial, but these two have had theirs too long for us to change them."

She clapped her hands to cut through the general chat that had started up.

"That's the good bit," she said, "and it's very good indeed because they'll make the farm more interesting and they'll earn their keep. We'll start a one-pony riding school with Polka and we'll also be able to charge a modest amount for visitors to ride Dot – you volunteers ride free, of course. But . . . but . . ."

She had to raise her voice because the room had all at once become extremely noisy.

"But . . . there is a small problem. They can't come until we can provide stabling for them."

"Can't the man who owns them do that?" said Seth. "If we're looking after them."

"We'll be the owners," said Jenny. "He's giving them to us, entirely free. He could easily have sold them. We can't expect him to do any more. The thing is, as long as we get enough strong volunteers – and some of the adults who come on different days have already offered – we can do the building ourselves, with the help of George's know-how." She looked directly at Kate. "You don't know how this place works yet, do you, Kate?" she said. "The thing

is, three of us are full-time and although we all do
everything, we've each had different training. I'm
'beasts', Mike's 'plants' and George" — she waved
her hand at the other man — "is 'buildings'."

"You may not think I've built much, yet," said
George rather sadly to Kate, "but materials cost
money, and we tend to be a bit short of that."

Kate, who wasn't sure she liked so much attention,
sat up straight and nodded fiercely to show that she
understood and that they didn't need to go on
explaining.

"We always seem to need extra money for
something," said Jenny, talking to everybody again,
not just Kate, who slumped gratefully back into a
more comfortable position, "but right now, stabling
takes priority. The first thing we've decided to do is
to have a Summer Open Day, and what I want from

you lot are IDEAS. As you know, we haven't got an awful lot here to show people yet, so we're going to need all sorts of events, and stalls, and unusual things that'll draw people in and bring in the loot."

"Fortune-teller," said one of the girls.

Jenny made a face.

"Rides on Polka and Dot," said one of the boys.

"They're too far away to come for the day," said Jenny. "They can't come until they can stay, so we can't include them. Give yourselves time to think and let's have your thoughts next Saturday, OK?"

She jumped down from the table and went off to fill up the water-bucket for the geese.

Mike came over to Kate. "Ready to milk Cleopatra?" he said, and walked away, indicating that she should follow him.

Dan stopped her in the doorway. "Are you sure you wouldn't rather milk the sheep?" he said, with a smug smile.

Kate looked up at him. She knew you got wool from sheep, not milk, and she very nearly said so. But on the other hand it wasn't long since she'd 'known' that goats were white and pigs were pink – and Dan did have a very peculiar expression on his face.

She thought quickly and played safe. "You can milk the sheep if you want," she said. "I'm promised to Cleopatra."

Dan looked briefly puzzled, then shrugged and went on his way.

Later, as Cleopatra stood peaceably on a small table in one of the sheds and Kate sat on the table's edge, leaning against the coarse-haired shoulder and squeezing the udder under Mike's direction, she said, "Do people milk sheep?"

"We do," said Mike. "Ours are British Frieslands – good for milk as well as wool. Dan's going to milk them in a minute, I think, as soon as he's cleaned out the pigs."

4 The Amazing Idea

"You don't have to go to the farm tomorrow," said Kate's mother on Friday, "as it's School Sports Day today. Not if you're tired."

"I have to go at least one more time," said Kate, "or Dan will think I've stayed away because I'm too young."

"Does anyone from school go?" said her mother.

"No," said Kate. "Hardly anyone at all goes, as far as I can see."

"It could be quite a nice little small-holding when they get it working properly," said her father.

"Where are Mike and Jenny from, did they say?"

"They're local," said Kate. "Everyone's local. Mike's father runs the Betting Shop in Wakeman

Street. Jenny went to my school when she was young. She says they used to have a big Sports Day for the whole school then, not separate ones for each class like now. She says it took ages and she remembers getting very hot."

Her father's mind was still on the farm that afternoon when he and her mother arrived at the School Field. "If Jenny and Mike are local people," he said to Kate as she showed them to their seats, "who really runs the farm?"

"They do," said Kate, hitching her shorts and wondering if she would be able to remember which leg went first over the high jump.

e to start a farm," said her
o know what's what."
s," said Kate. "Like yours,
pigs, not computers. I have to
e first race."

"Good ... her mother.

"Thank you," said Kate, "but these Sports are 'non-competitive', Mr Bolton says."

"Someone has to win," said her mother.

"Yes," said Kate, "but it's not meant to matter who."

"Farming's in the blood," said her father. "I think you'll find some countryman's behind it all."

"I'll ask," said Kate and went to the starting line for the sprint.

She finished middle, a neat position she felt.

Later she noticed with satisfaction that her place in all the events was the same, not first nor last but exactly middle – until it came to the Obstacle Race called Getting to Work.

At the shout of 'GO', everyone had to run to a heap of clothes and put on a hat, a coat and a pair of gloves. Each button had to be fastened on the coat, each finger had to be in the right bit of glove. Most of the class managed this in the time allowed. Mr Bolton, who was standing at the end with a stop watch, shouted out that they had caught the commuter train and could run straight for the finishing line.

He told the rest, Kate among them, that they had missed the train and had to get to work on foot. This was where the real obstacles started. The route they had to take was through a tunnel of car tyres, propped on their sides, up a short ladder, across a narrow plank, down the ladder the other side, in and out of six markers which were stuck in the ground inconveniently close to each other, and finally up and over a small mountain made of three benches and the vaulting horse from the gym, two strong packing cases, and a cleverly balanced rocking plank.

The rule was one at a time for each obstacle, which meant that an agitated queue of weirdly dressed people built up behind each one.

"Come on!" called Mr Bolton to Kate, perhaps forgetting about the race being non-competitive. "Get into the spirit of it. You're in a hurry. You're a person who's missed the train and is taking a short cut to work."

Well, I must be a very stupid person, thought Kate, as she minced up a sloping bench onto the back of the vaulting horse, her too-long coat buttoned wrongly and her too-large hat slipping over her eyes. "Why don't I just catch the next train?"

Trying not to be put off by all the puffing and gasping and sounds of ripping coat hems behind her, she negotiated the rocking bench on the other side of the horse – tipping it down towards her before she started to walk along it, and then tipping it down away from her when she reached the middle. No one but a goat would go to work this way, she thought.

She finished last and her parents hurried up to tell her she mustn't mind.

"I don't," said Kate, unbuttoning the big coat but still thinking about goats. "I only mind that I'm too hot. If it was worse than this when Jenny was my age I don't know why they didn't all die."

"Everyone in your class seems very nice," said her mother brightly.

"Yes," said Kate, thinking that they were much nicer than one or two she could mention down on the farm. But, she said to herself, it'll be all right tomorrow, because I've had an Amazing Idea.

5   Animal Sports Day

Kate had to clench her toes inside her shoes to make herself stand up and speak at the farm meeting next day, but she managed it.

"I've had an idea for Open Day," she said.

"Let's hear it," said Jenny.

"Animal Sports Day!" said Kate.

There was a blank silence for a moment and then Dan said, "Oh yeah! I'll do the posters. Pole-vaulting pigs! Hurdling hens!"

There was an explosion of laughter from the rest of the Junior Farmers' Club, and Seth said loudly, "Trust her!"

"All right, all right," said Jenny. "Now let's think a minute."

"Is there any more to your idea, Kate?" said Mike. He looked a bit mystified, but he wasn't laughing, and neither were Jenny or George.

Kate could feel that her face had become very red, which for some reason had an odd effect on her voice. It came out very high-pitched, much higher than her father's had when he'd warned her about the Gander attack. But then, to be fair to it, it started higher in the first place. She kept going by fixing her eyes on Mike's kind, toy-monkey face and ignoring everyone else. She explained about the Getting to Work race at school, and how she'd thought they could perhaps set up a Goat Obstacle Course for the kids in much the same way, but with no hats and coats.

"And no kid gloves?" said Dan, but he didn't sound as scornful as he had before, and the others had quietened down again.

"It could work," said Mike.

"I've heard of a farm where they race pigs," said Jenny. "I think they use three- to four-month-old ones — ours'd be about right."

Alison, who hadn't said anything yet, was looking doubtful. "There'll be objections," she said, "on the grounds of cruelty."

"Oh, we wouldn't be cruel," said Kate, horrified, and not wanting Alison to disapprove of her. "We wouldn't make them do anything they didn't want. The kids *like* climbing obstacles, that's why I thought of it."

"But how do you make pigs race?" said Alison, who still looked a bit unhappy.

"I know the theory," said Jenny. "Instead of feeding them in the sty, you put the trough outside. And each day you move it a little farther away. They get the best possible reward for running, and the exercise is good for them. All right, Alison?"

"That sounds all right," Alison agreed.

"There'd have to be a gate," said Dan, "that we could pull up quickly, to give them all a fair start."

"That could be managed," said George.

"And we'd have to get some washable paint in different colours to identify them with," said Mike. "Whatever Dan thinks, hardly anyone can tell them apart by their markings."

"Right, then," said Jenny. "I think we can say Animal Sports Day is officially on the agenda."

"Neat!" said Liz, with the spiky hair and the bat

ear-ring. "Really neat!"

Seth looked at Dan. "OK, I expect we can make it work," he said.

Before the meeting broke up it was agreed that, without a sheep dog, there wasn't much ewes could do, and anyway they were booked to take part in a shearing demonstration. The hens, though, or anyway some of them, were to compete in a treasure hunt. The 'treasure' – a bright yellow rectangle of cardboard with the word 'GOLD' printed on it – would be covered with gravel and corn and the audience would bet on which hen would scratch it up first.

Liz volunteered to make the different ~~~ bands.

Dan agreed that he really would do the posters. "What'll we call the events?" he said. "The Incredible Kid Climb?"

"Good," said Mike. "And the Great Pig Trot."

"That sounds like a huge foot," said Kate, no longer nervous of speaking. "Can't it be The Great Pig Sprint?"

The geese were let off on the grounds of ill-temper, which was just as well because not long after the meeting Gander got out of his pen and menaced Seth, cornering him near the disapproving goats.

"That's weird," everyone agreed, as they drove Gander off and helped George repair the fence. "Seth's good with animals, Gander's always OK with Seth."

Kate went over to Cleopatra and put her arms round her neck. "Seth," she whispered into Cleopatra's floppy ear, "has just as much trouble with Gander as anyone else. Why does he get sympathy and I got laughed at? That IS weird." Cleopatra pressed her head against Kate's and sent comforting goat-thoughts into her brain.

The pigs had their first training session at the end of the afternoon. The trough was positioned two feet from the sty gate. The gate was opened, but the entrance was blocked by a piece of hardboard held on one side by Mike and on the other by George.

Alison brought the swill bucket to the trough and filled it noisily.

The young pigs crowded behind the hardboard.

Jenny gave the signal.

George and Mike lifted the board and eight small bodies hurtled at the food in a solid line.

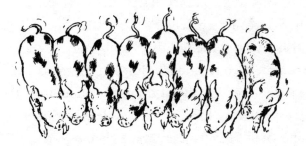

"They all won," said Kate. "I'm not sure people'll bet money if it's going to be as non-competitive as this."

"Remember we move the trough farther away each day," said Jenny. "When the track is longer, I think we'll get a clear winner."

"They're fast, though," said Kate, anxiously. "This race is going to be over very quickly, isn't it?"

"About thirty seconds, I reckon," said Jenny.

"Will people be impressed by that?" said Kate.

"If I do a nice big 'build-up' announcement, I think they will," said Jenny. "And we can stage more than one race. Open Day lasts from two till five, so I think we can fit in three. After that the pigs'll have had enough."

"Tired," said Kate sympathetically.

"No," said Jenny, "full."

"What's to go on this poster, then," said Dan. "I'd better start this weekend."

"I'll give you the full list," said Jenny. "We've got lots of more conventional things lined up, as well as the sheep-shearing. But I think you should use the biggest lettering for The Incredible Kid Climb, The Stupendous Hen Treasure Scratch and – the highlight of the day – The Great Pig Sprint."

6 The Great Pig Sprint

Parked cars glinted in the sun all along the road.

A banner, with 'LEE ROAD CITY FARM OPEN DAY' painted on it in red, was stretched along the fence.

Behind it, the farmyard was almost unrecognisable. Mike was in charge of a brightly coloured inflated castle near the gate, which bulged and rocked as the younger visitors bounded about on it. Sometimes, to stop himself feeling seasick, he looked instead at the red wooden box with the slot in the top which was wired to the fence beside him. A notice taped to the front of the box read: 'Voluntary Entrance Fee. We Suggest 20p (But Don't Let That Stop You Putting In More).' The weight of coins was already making it hang crooked. Below the red box a large piece of white cardboard was propped against the fence. Pasted on to it were four photographs of Polka and Dot. Across the top of it was written: 'PLEASE HELP TO BUY US A STABLE'.

There were several stalls scattered about. Dan in his Save The Whale T-shirt and Liz with her bat ear-ring swinging ran the busiest one, selling milk, cheese, eggs, lettuces and radishes from Lee Road Farm itself. The home-made jam and cakes were in demand, too, and bric-a-brac and books weren't doing badly. A boy called Matthew and a girl called

Gloria were taking turns to stand near Gander's pen and suggest to people that it was a bad idea to climb into it.

A patient saddle-maker was producing the slowest saddle of his entire career, letting every passing child put in a stitch. A man from Chapel Street City Farm was having an easy time of it, putting on a sheep-shearing demonstration every half-hour. ("We've only got five," Mike had said, "so don't work too fast.") A woman from the same farm was working a lot harder, giving unceasing spinning lessons and selling spindles at the same time ('Half the proceeds to Lee Road Farm').

However, the day was not without its problems.

"I think the goat-kids' performance has suffered from over-attention to the pigs," said Kate. She chose to speak formally because one or two from her class had turned up with their parents, and looked quite impressed to see her so well established.

George had built a beautiful Kid Climb Course in the fenced enclosure; that wasn't the problem.

Alison, Seth and Matthew were very patient about getting the three contestants down one end of it and then releasing them at Jenny's shout; that wasn't the problem either.

The problem was that, once released, the kids turned out to be enthusiastic but completely undisciplined. They liked their Obstacle Course all right, but they liked their audience better, especially when it laughed and clapped. They skipped and sprang and flirted around the edges of the enclosure, letting out giggling bleats. The watching children giggled and bleated back and the goat kids skipped higher.

When Alison, Seth and Matthew caught them again, and pushed them right AT their mini-mountain of crates and planks, the kids tried a new diversion. Charmian's daughter ran straight to the top and tip-toed about, pretending she didn't know how to get down, while the other two began to spring high off the ground, their front legs drawn up tight and their back legs stretched out straight, and to twist right round in the air before landing.

"Is that what we expected them to do?" said George, watching the display of spinning leaps.

"Not exactly," said Kate. "Well – not at all, really."

"Maybe we should have had a band," said George,

"and called it Kid Country Dancing."

The pigs, who had run their first race of the day at the very beginning of the afternoon, had behaved very differently. When their gate had been lifted they had headed for their distant trough without a moment's hesitation, heads lowered, trotters twinkling, totally unaware of the numerous distractions around them.

Two Stupendous Hen Treasure Scratches had been staged, each of them reasonably successful, although the hens were a bit slow and fussy about it all and cackled rather irritatingly throughout.

But the kids, it had to be admitted, were a

complete failure. Even Charmian and Blondie, watching from their stables, turned their heads away as if in embarrassment, and Cleopatra comforted herself by gnawing thoughtfully on the top of her half-door with her eyes closed.

Eventually, Jenny announced that the first Kid Climb was scrubbed. The Second Kid Climb, she promised, would be announced later on, when the participants had calmed down a bit. She also said that all the people who'd placed bets could have their money back, but luckily no one wanted that.

"The kids were my first and best idea," said Kate sadly.

"Keep your mind on the pigs," said George. "The pigs are OK."

Which was true at first.

Amelia, running with a red marker, had won the opening Pig Sprint easily. Abel, in second place, only just had his snout level with her flank when her own was already deep in the swill. Kate's father had bet on Amelia, handing over his money to Mike's father, who did not have a beard nor, as it happened, any hair. Kate's teacher, Mr Bolton, had put money on Abel, and Mrs Bolton had fancied Ada, but being non-competitive people they hadn't minded losing. In fact they'd gone straight to Abigail's sty afterwards to tell her what a fast litter she had.

Before the second Pig Sprint, an hour or so later, George and Jenny discreetly washed off the marks and recoloured the pigs. Mike's father took up his position and announced himself ready to receive bets. "Put your money on the winner, put your money on the loser, put your money on whatever you like as long as you give it to me," he shouted.

The trough was refilled. The spectators gathered.

Afterwards there were all sorts of different suggestions about what had gone wrong, but most people agreed to put the blame on Adeline, Arnold, and also on whoever had got their trotters in the trough the first time round.

Adeline and Arnold, already famous as fast eaters, had devoured so much at the end of the first race that their appetites had not fully recovered in time for the second. It wasn't that they minded eating again, it was just that they thought it would be fun to chat to a few spectators on the way.

While they jogged outwards, to the delight of the race-goers, Amy – not five seconds after the start – discovered a small pile of delicious swill in mid-track, obviously dropped by a returning trotter after Sprint number one. She stooped to enjoy it and Alban collided with her and knocked her sideways into the path of Aylmer, who fell over her. Aylmer got up quickly, but facing in the wrong direction. Amy, having polished off her extra treat, set off again at some speed, overtook the trough, turned in a cloud of dust and came at it from the wrong side. At the same time Aylmer spun himself round to face the right way and began again, but, finding Abel in front of him, got confused and thought he was supposed to be chasing him. As Abel had, at that moment, decided to chase Amy, this meant that he and Aylmer also ended up beyond the winning trough. By the time they turned back they were almost the

last, apart from Adeline and Arnold who had
suddenly remembered that the last to reach the food
doesn't find much, and had hurtled in from the
outside of the track.

Amelia, meanwhile, racing this time in a black
marker, had ignored all the snorting confusion and
gone straight for the swill, an easy first once more.

To Kate's surprise, this second Pig Sprint got a
much louder cheer than the first one. Before she
could work out why, Dan, who had left the stall to
watch, strolled past saying, "Your dad's not bad.
He's won again. He knows Amelia by her
markings."

At that point Jenny announced the second Kid
Climb, which meant that a lot of people were

watching when Alison, going into the enclosure to try and impose a little order, accidentally let the over-excited Golden Guernsey kid escape.

The kid skittered away at speed and the more people joined in the chase, the faster it ran. It reached the outer gate just as a woman with an enormous shopping basket was coming in. Lowering its small blonde head it ran out under cover of the basket. It was so quick that she didn't notice it go, and was a little disconcerted to see a considerable number of people running straight at her, shouting.

Outside, faced with a wall of parked cars, the kid tried to climb onto the bonnet of a blue Fiat. Seth reached it and caught it in his arms just in time. Half a second later Alison, Mike, Jenny, Dan and the rest of the pursuers arrived at the farm gate. Kate, who had wriggled her way through the crowd to the front, stopped dead – and so did everyone else.

There was a dent in the wing of the Fiat, quite a big dent, finished off at the top with two neat little scratches, made by two neat little hooves.

There was a moment of horrified silence.

Kate thought, all the money we've made today will have to go to fix the car. Then she wondered if that would be enough, and for a nightmare moment she imagined Dan telling her that the farm would have to be sold, to pay for a new car – and that it was all her fault.

Before anyone could speak, Mr Bolton stepped forward and patted the car on its roof in a possessive way.

"Oh I AM sorry," said Alison, who looked as if she might cry.

But Mr Bolton smiled, a rather fixed smile, and laughed, a rather strained laugh, and said, "Never mind, I think scratches give a car character. I declare this kid the winner!"

Everybody else laughed too – most of them, including Kate, more with relief than amusement. They went back in through the gate and shut it. Seth took the kicking kid back to the pen, remarking that these Sports were getting a bit too exciting. Mike explained matters to the bewildered woman with the basket. Alison apologised again, and Jenny said to Mr Bolton, "You're really being VERY good about this."

"Oh well," said Mr Bolton, his smile becoming a little less fixed, "I have to confess the dent was there already. My son is going to hammer it out for me

this weekend, and I'm secretly hoping he'll touch up the scratches at the same time."

"That was nearly a disaster," said Kate, when she rejoined her parents.

"But it's all right now," said her mother. "I think the whole day's been a great success."

"Great fun," said her father, "but not a total success."

"Why not?" said Kate.

"They can't have raised enough to build a double stable out of the small sums they've taken this afternoon," said her father.

Kate, who had spent all morning helping to set up stalls, and all afternoon worrying about kids and pigs, and selling jam while the jam lady went off to learn to spin, suddenly felt very tired.

"Are you sure?" she said.

"Afraid so," said her father. Her mother said something reassuring, but Kate didn't listen, she ran over to Mike, who was talking to his own father.

"This is the first time in my working life," Mike's father was saying, "that only two winners took their money. And even they went and put it in the red box. You'll have to take some of this bunce off me, it's weighing me down."

As he wandered off, leaving Mike with his money pouch, Kate said, "My father says we're not going to raise enough for the stables, is that right, and also I keep forgetting to ask, are you from the country?"

"No," said Mike, looking a bit surprised. "I'm from here."

"My father," said Kate, "doesn't think people can be farmers unless they were born in the country."

"I see," said Mike. "But you don't have to be born down a volcano to know how to light a fire, do you?"

"Oh," said Kate. "No. I'll tell him. But what about the money?"

"There won't be enough here," said Mike, rattling the money pouch, "but three of today's visitors liked the farm so much they've made donations. We've got enough for the stables already, and we haven't counted this or the red box yet."

"You didn't need Animal Sports Day then!" said Kate.

"We did," said Mike, "indeed we did. That's what made people come in the first place."

"But the races mostly went wrong," wailed Kate.

"People LOVE it when things go wrong," said Mike.

"Everyone's had a really good time today."

"Not my teacher," said Kate, "not Mr Bolton, whose car was scratched."

"He's had the best time," said Mike. "He was nice about it so everybody thinks what a good sort he is and he can feel pleased about himself for days. So can you – you've been a terrific help. Even Dan thinks so, though he may not tell you himself."

"So the pony and donkey can come?"

"As soon as the work's done."

"The only thing I know about ponies and donkeys," said Kate, "is that one end bites and the other end kicks."

"Sit in the middle where it's safe, then," said Mike, "and learn to ride."

"I might try it once," said Kate guardedly. "But if either of them throws me off, I'm not having another go."